Inside a House That Is Haunted

For Billy with love
—A.S.C.

To Matthew, Justin, and Joshua
—T.A.

Text copyright © 1998 by Alyssa Satin Capucilli.
Illustrations copyright © 1998 by Tedd Arnold.

All rights reserved. Published by Scholastic Inc.
SCHOLASTIC, CARTWHEEL BOOKS, and associated logos
are trademarks and/or registered trademarks of Scholastic Inc.
Lexile is a registered trademark of MetaMetrics, Inc.

Library of Congress Cataloging-in-Publication Data is available.

ISBN 978-0-545-28734-0

12 11 10   14 15 16 17 18 19/0

Printed in the U.S.A.   40
This edition first printing, July 2011

Inside a House That Is Haunted

By Alyssa Satin Capucilli
Illustrated by Tedd Arnold

SCHOLASTIC INC.

Here is a house that is haunted.

Here is the hand that knocked
on the door
outside a house that is haunted.

Here is the hand that knocked
on the door

and startled the spider that
dropped to the floor
inside a house that is haunted.

Here is the hand that knocked
on the door
and startled the spider that
dropped to the floor

that frightened the ghost who
awoke and cried, "BOO!"
inside a house that is haunted.

Here is the hand that knocked
on the door
and startled the spider that
dropped to the floor
that frightened the ghost who
awoke and cried, "BOO!"

surprising the cat that
jumped and screeched, "MEW!"
inside a house that is haunted.

Here is the hand that knocked
on the door
and startled the spider that
dropped to the floor
that frightened the ghost who
awoke and cried, "BOO!"
surprising the cat that
jumped and screeched, "MEW!"

that shook up the bats that
swooped through the air
inside a house that is haunted.

Here is the hand that knocked
on the door
and startled the spider that
dropped to the floor
that frightened the ghost who
awoke and cried, "BOO!"
surprising the cat that
jumped and screeched, "MEW!"
that shook up the bats that
swooped through the air

and jolted the owl that called,
"Who—Who's there?"
inside a house that is haunted.

Here is the hand that knocked
on the door
and startled the spider that
dropped to the floor
that frightened the ghost who
awoke and cried, "BOO!"
surprising the cat that
jumped and screeched, "MEW!"
that shook up the bats that
swooped through the air
and jolted the owl that
called, "Who—Who's there?"

that spooked the mummy who
ran with a shriek
inside a house that is haunted.

Here is the hand that knocked
on the door
and startled the spider that
dropped to the floor
that frightened the ghost who
awoke and cried, "BOO!"
surprising the cat that
jumped and screeched, "MEW!"
that shook up the bats that
swooped through the air
and jolted the owl that
called, "Who—Who's there?"
that spooked the mummy who
ran with a shriek

rattling the skeleton who
moved with a creak
inside a house that is haunted.

Here is the hand that knocked
on the door

and startled the spider that
dropped to the floor

that frightened the ghost who
awoke and cried, "BOO!"

surprising the cat that
jumped and screeched, "MEW!"

that shook up the bats that
swooped through the air

and jolted the owl that
called, "Who—Who's there?"

that spooked the mummy who
ran with a shriek

rattling the skeleton who
moved with a creak

that

WOKE

the monster

who stomped on huge feet…

threw open the door
and heard "TRICK OR TREAT!"

INSIDE A HOUSE THAT IS HAUNTED.